SOMEONE NEW

AN URSULA NORDSTROM BOOK

Charlotte Zolotow

SOMEONE NEW

With illustrations by
Erik Blegvad

HarperCollins*Publishers*

Someone New
Text copyright © 1978 by Charlotte Zolotow
Illustrations copyright © 1978 by Erik Blegvad
All rights reserved. No part of this book may be used or
reproduced in any manner whatsoever without written
permission except in the case of brief quotations embodied
in critical articles and reviews. Printed in Mexico.
For information address HarperCollins Children's Books,
a division of HarperCollins Publishers,
10 East 53rd Street, New York, NY 10022.

Library of Congress Cataloging-in-Publication Data
Zolotow, Charlotte Shapiro, date
  Someone new.

  "An Ursula Nordstrom book."
  Summary: A youngster discovers changes within
himself as he matures and acquires new interests.
  I. Blegvad, Erik. II. Title.
PZ7.Z77Sp   [E]   77-11838
ISBN 0-06-027017-9
ISBN 0-06-027018-7 (lib. bdg.)

For Allie

I have this feeling

someone is gone
and I don't know who.

My mother is here.
My father is here.
My sister is here.
Who is gone?

I lie on my bed and look at the wallpaper.
I chose the wallpaper in my room last year.
It has red and blue balloons.
There was another paper that looked like wood.

I wish I had chosen that.
Something is strange.
I don't like this wallpaper anymore.

I go downstairs.
The banister is worn and smooth.
The rugs and the books and the plants
are in their right place
but
something is different.
Someone isn't here.
I don't know who.

The doorbell rings,
one short and two long.
It's my friend, Jack.
"Hi," he says.
"Hi," I say.
"Do you want to come out?" he says.
I say,
"What will we do?"
"Want to play marbles?"
I like to shoot marbles.
"No," I say.
"What do you want to do?" he says.
"Walk?" I say.

So we take a walk.
Jack is with me

but someone is missing,
and I don't know who.

Back home,
Jack says,
"What about this afternoon?"
"I don't know yet," I say
and close the door.

My sister
is playing with blocks.
She likes me to build for her.

When I get the last block on top,
she knocks them all down
and laughs.
I like to hear her laugh.

"Build?" she says.
"No," I say
and go upstairs.

I go into my room.
The balloons are floating on the wall.
The bed is made.
Bear and Panda are sitting on it
with their arms reaching out.

I push the arms down.
I look at my shelves.
Books and bottle caps
and baseball cards
and the box of shells
from one summer at the beach.

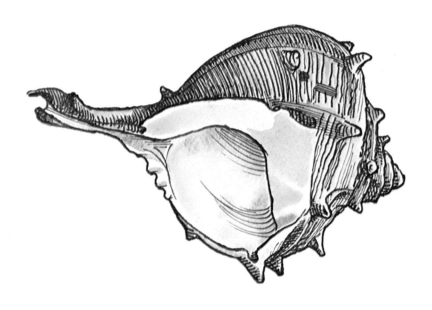

I pick up a shell.
It has a twisted shape
and is pink and white and grey.

I take up each shell
one by one
and arrange them on my bureau.
I stare at them.

I never really looked at them before.
I never thought about them,
how they were washed up from the sea,
what lived in them.

I remember the summer at the beach.
I wish I could go back now.
I would find out about the shells.

I look around the room at all the junk,
games, bottle caps, Bear and Panda,

26

as though they belong
to someone else.

I get a grocery carton
and pack up everything
except some books
and the shells.
Even Bear and Panda.
I want them out of my room.

I'm glad I'm not seeing Jack later.
I want to go to the library.
I want a book on shells.

I look at the box of things
I'm sending out of my room.
Panda's arm is sticking up.
The feeling I have is sad
but happy too.

Someone's gone.
Someone's missing
and I know who.

He's in that box
with all those things
and I —
I am someone new.